STONE Soup

A Folk Tale to Find the Meaning and a Soup Recipe

Written by Rich Linville
ISBN: 9781797990743

I am a poor, wandering hobo with nothing in my pockets.

I see a smooth round stone by the river bank and pick it up.

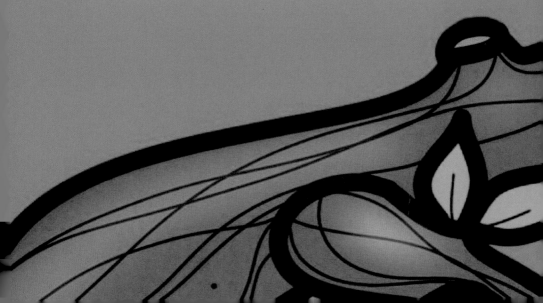

It's a cold, windy day. There's a house. I hope that they can spare some food for a hungry hobo.

Burrr! It's cold. I will politely tap on the front door.

A family comes outside. The Father says, "I'm sorry. We have no food for strangers."

I say, "If you will let me borrow a cooking pot and spoon, I will make some stone soup for you and your family."

With a puzzled look, the Father places a cooking pot on the ground and pours clean water into the pot. He hands me a spoon.

I wash and clean the rock. Using the spoon, I place the rock in the pot.

The Father starts his kindling on fire using two flint stones. Then, he places logs on top of the burning kindling. Finally, he puts his pot of water on the flaming logs.

After tasting the rock soup, I say that it needs carrots to improve the taste.

The Mother brings carrots to me.

I tell her that carrots have a sweet, fruity flavor.
They are healthy and add taste and vitamin A to the soup. Vitamin A improves your vision.

The Daughter brings onions to me.

Onions give a delicious bite or sharp flavor to soup. They are high in vitamins and minerals.

After tasting, I say that it needs celery to improve it.

The Son brings celery to me.

Despite it's nearly flavorless taste, celery is rich in vitamins, minerals and fiber.

The Father brings garlic and other spices to me.

I explain that garlic and other spices lend flavor to the broth. I remove the stone and put it in my pocket.

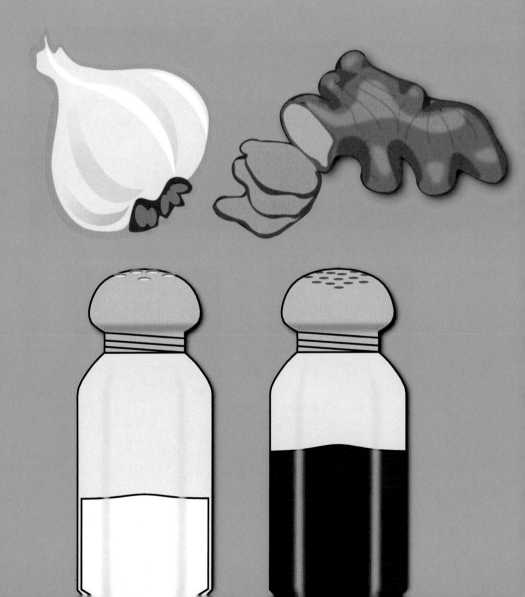

At an outside table, we share our delicious stone soup.

This is not the end. It's the beginning of delicious meals.

Which of these do you think is the meaning, moral or lesson of this folk tale?

❑ 1. This is a moral regarding the value and importance of sharing.

❑ 2. The theme is that people benefit from contributing.

❑ 3. The best meals are shared by all.

❑ 4. I, myself, think it means ...

Folk tales can have meanings that are not the same for different people. Any of these are possible answers

☐ 1. This is a moral regarding the value and importance of sharing.

☐ 2. The theme is that people benefit from contributing.

☐ 3. The best meals are shared by all.

☐ 4. I, myself, think it means ...

**Recipe for
Homemade Soup
Note: Please do not use
real stones in your soup.
You might
break your teeth!**

Homemade Soup
Materials Needed

❑ 1. Vegetable, Meat Broth or Water

❑ 2. Pan for cooking on stove

Some Vegetables like

❑ 3. carrots or celery

❑ 4. onions or garlic

❑ 5. leeks or green beans

❑ 6. asparagus or green peas

❑ 7. other fresh vegetables

Some Herbs in Small Amounts

❑ 7. parsley or bay leaf

❑ 8. oregano or dill or basil

Steps to Make Your Soup
Part One

❑ 1. Chop vegetables small to maximize the flavors. One-half inch (1 centimeter) cubes are a good size. You can use a food processor to make the pieces.

❑ 2. Lightly brown the vegetables by roasting to bring out more flavors.

❑ 3. Add cold water to a soup Pan. Starting with cold water and slowly increasing the stove top temperature helps to give more flavors. Do not start with warm or hot water.

❑ 4. Turn heat to medium and slowly bring to just under a boil. Add spices to your taste.

Steps to Make Your Soup
Part Two

❏ 5. Reduce the heat and keep at a simmer with a few bubbles around the edge of the soup. Do not allow the soup to boil or you will lose flavors.

❏ 6. Do not stir or the vegetables will break down into mush.

❏ 7. Cook for less than 1 ½ hours. Cooking too long will lose flavors.

❏ 8. Allow to cool.

❏ 9. Enjoy your homemade vegetable soup.

Dedicated to my lovely wife
Sulastri and my grandchildren
Mia and Kai as well as everyone
who enjoys folk tales.

For over 40 years, I have
enjoyed teaching at elementary,
high school and college levels.

I would love to hear from you.
You can email me at
richardvlinville@gmail.com

Illustrations from OpenClipArt,
PixaBay, Wiki, and illustrations
purchased from Edu-Clips.com.

Please check out
my other books
at bookstores
and online
under the name
Rich Linville.

My Alaskan Race
by Huskie Dog

From my point of view

Written by Rich Linville

My Basketball Blues
from the Basketball's Point of View
Written by Rich Linville

My Rocky Adventure!
By Rocky Magma
Written by Rich Linville

Someday I'd like to be
a rock instead of magma

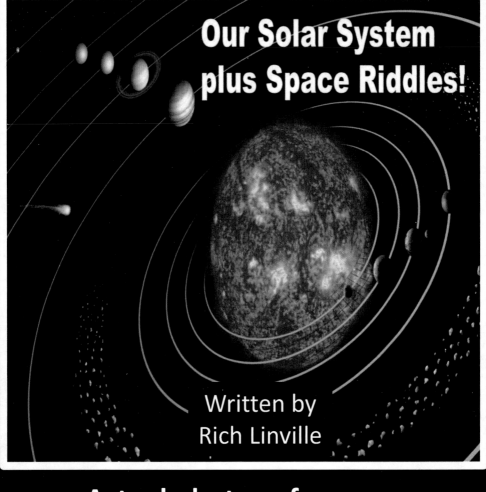

Our Solar System plus Space Riddles!

Written by
Rich Linville

Actual photos of our sun, planets and a dwarf planet. Learn about our solar system with a trick to remember the order of the planets.